# SCREAM STREET

## Book Four

## FLESH OF THE ZOMBIE

# SCREAM STREET

## Book Four
## FLESH OF THE ZOMBIE

# TOMMY D🕱NBAVAND

**CANDLEWICK PRESS**

Text copyright © 2008 by Tommy Donbavand
Illustrations copyright © 2008 by Cartoon Saloon Ltd.

First U.S. edition 2010

Library of Congress Cataloging-in-Publication Data

Donbavand, Tommy.
Flesh of the zombie / by Tommy Donbavand. —1st ed.
p.   cm. — (Scream Street ; 4)
Summary: Deadstock, the world's greatest zombie rock festival, comes to Scream Street, but when the headlining band is banished to the evil Underlands and townsfolk riot, Luke and his friends must restore peace if they plan to continue their search for the relics that will allow Luke to return home.
ISBN 978-0-7636-4637-0
[1. Horror stories.  2. Zombies—Fiction.  3. Werewolves—Fiction.
4. Rock groups—Fiction.]  I. Title.  II. Series.
PZ7.D7162Fl 2010
[Fic]—dc22      2009039356

10 11 12 13 14 15 SOL 10 9 8 7 6 5 4 3 2

Printed in Scott Junction, Quebec, Canada

This book was typeset in Bembo Educational.
The illustrations were done in ink.

Candlewick Press
99 Dover Street
Somerville, Massachusetts 02144

visit us at www.candlewick.com

For Arran, who wanted to be a
zombie rock drummer called Twonk

# Meet the residents

Luke Watson

Cleo Farr

Resus Negative

Dixon

Sir Otto Sneer

Samuel Skipstone

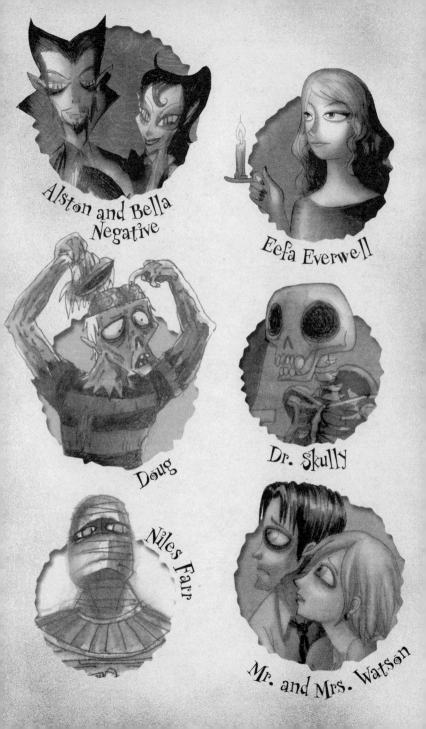

Alston and Bella Negative

Eefa Everwell

Doug

Dr. Skully

Niles Farr

Mr. and Mrs. Watson

# Welcome to Scream Street

# Who lives where

**A** Sneer Hall

**B** Central Square

**C** Everwell's Emporium

**D** No. 2: The Crudleys

**E** No. 5: The Movers

**F** No. 11: Twinkle

**G** No. 13: Luke Watson

**H** No. 14: Resus Negative

**I** No. 21: Eefa Everwell

**J** No. 22: Cleo Farr

**K** No. 28: Doug, Turf, and Berry

**L** No. 32: Simon Howl

**M** No. 39: The Skullys

# Previously on Scream Street . . .

Luke Watson was a perfectly ordinary boy until his tenth birthday, when he transformed into a werewolf. After it happened two more times, Luke and his family were forcibly moved by G.H.O.U.L. (Government Housing of Unusual Life-forms) to Scream Street, a community of ghosts, monsters, zombies, and more.

Luke quickly found his feet, making friends with Cleo Farr (a headstrong mummy) and Resus Negative, the son of the vampires next door. Luke soon realized, however, that Mr. and Mrs. Watson would never get over their fear of their nightmarish neighbors. With the help of an ancient book, *Skipstone's Tales of Scream Street,* he set out to find six relics, each left behind by one of the community's founding fathers. Only their combined power will enable him to open a doorway out of Scream Street and take his parents home.

Luke is now halfway through his quest, having already located a vampire's fang, a vial of witch's blood, and the heart of an ancient mummy. To locate the fourth artifact, however, Luke, Resus, and Cleo will have to travel deep underground. . . .

# Chapter One
# The Zombies

**Luke Watson** stared at the length of spine on the grass in front of him and frowned in concentration. Biology lessons at his old school had never been like this.

"Well?" asked Dr. Skully. "Can you, or can you not, indicate where the lumbar section starts and ends?"

Luke briefly wondered whether he should be more surprised that he was being taught by a skeleton or that it was the teacher's own detached backbone he was examining. Since he had arrived in Scream Street, however, surprises like this had become an everyday occurrence, so neither fact seemed that strange now.

Daylight had only just returned to Scream Street after a century-old darkness spell had been broken. As a result, today's class was taking place in Dr. Skully's backyard—and while the surroundings were comfortable, Luke found it difficult to concentrate in such a casual atmosphere.

"I'm waiting," said the teacher.

"I, er . . ." began Luke.

A clatter from the patio provided a welcome distraction. "It's no good, sir," complained a small Egyptian mummy. "I can't reassemble your ribs!"

"Cleo, please be careful with those," Dr. Skully said with a sigh. "The last time I provided ribs for a pupil, he lost three of them and my pajamas didn't fit for a month!"

"But, sir, I—"

The mummy squealed as she was interrupted by a fist punching up through the grass.

The young vampire sitting beside her grinned. "I've been waiting for this."

A cracked green face appeared through the widening hole, its milky eyes blinking in the sunlight. "Looking for something, Doug?" asked the vampire as he reached inside his cape and produced a leg, its skin covered with sores.

"Dude!" The zombie beamed. "I've been searching for that all morning."

"I found it on my way to school," said the vampire. "Heavy night?"

Doug nodded. "Party city, man! Now I got to get busy with the sewing kit. Big day today!" The zombie retrieved his missing limb and sank back into the hole. "Smell you later, little dudes."

The teacher's skull glared across the yard from its position on an upturned bucket. "Don't think your work with the undead will get you off the hook, Resus Negative!" it warned. "You still have the lower half of *my* leg to assemble."

"Why do we have to learn this stuff?" groaned Resus.

"Because," explained the skull, "I did not spend thirty years standing in the corner of a university science lab only to have the knowledge I gleaned go to waste!"

"But, sir," Resus said, grinning, "my brain's full—look!"

Luke fought back laughter as the vampire reached into the folds of his cape once again and produced a squishy gray organ coated in clear jelly.

"That's disgusting," moaned Cleo, gagging as she pulled her bandages up over her mouth.

"Whose brain is that?" demanded Dr. Skully.

"My great-uncle Igor sent it to me," replied Resus.

"Your family is sick!" said Cleo.

"How can *you* say that?" asked Resus. "You had your brain pulled out of your nose with metal hooks when you were mummified!"

"Maybe," said Cleo, "but I don't carry it around like some sort of troph—"

She screamed as another hand burst up through the grass in front of her.

Resus smiled. "What have you lost now, Doug?"

A gray head forced its way up through the earth. One of the creature's eyes was missing, and sticky brown fluid poured from a gash in its cheek.

 4

"Er, that's not Doug . . ." said Luke.

"Brain drain!" groaned the zombie, scanning the yard. "Brain drain!"

Resus jumped as another hand exploded through the lawn, followed by another a few feet away. More of the monsters appeared, digging their way out of the ground, all of them chanting the same phrase.

"Brain drain! Brain drain!"

"Eurgh," squealed Cleo. "Get them away from me!"

"What's the matter?" asked Resus. "They're only zombies."

"I just don't like them, that's all," Cleo said with a shiver as the creatures stumbled around the backyard. One of them staggered past her and landed with a splash in Dr. Skully's pond. Tiny skeletal fish darted for cover in the reeds.

"Will somebody please put a stop to this nonsense?" demanded Dr. Skully.

Resus approached the zombie nearest to him. "I think you've got the wrong address," he said, speaking loudly and slowly. "The only zombies in Scream Street live at number twenty-eight!"

"You think they're friends of Doug, Turf, and Berry?" asked Luke.

Resus shrugged. "Either that or they're tunneling north for the summer."

"Brain drain! Brain drain!" murmured the zombie.

"You're not draining *my* brain!" shouted Cleo, backing away. A pair of scabby gray arms grabbed the mummy, and the one-eyed zombie lifted her off her feet. Cleo squealed.

"Put her down," Luke ordered. The gray zombie squeezed Cleo tighter.

"Brain drain! Brain drain!"

"I said, put her down!" yelled Luke.

"Luke, behind you!" shouted Cleo.

Luke turned to find another zombie almost upon him. Snatching up Dr. Skully's spine from where it lay on the lawn, he hit the creature full in the face, knocking its head clean off its shoulders. The body collapsed to the ground, arms and legs twitching wildly.

"That'll teach you to *lumbar* after me," quipped Luke, grinning at his own joke and turning to give Resus a high five.

"But I don't get it," said the vampire, shaking his head. "Zombies don't normally act like this."

"Then we've obviously been watching different movies!"

"No, I mean, something's got them worked up. They're usually quite docile."

"Yeah," said Luke sarcastically. "Remind me to get one as a pet when this is over."

"When you two have finished chatting," called Cleo, wriggling in the grasp of the gray zombie, "can I remind you that I'm currently having the life squeezed out of me?"

"OK," Resus said, sighing and beginning to

search his cloak again. He produced a flaming torch, which he jabbed at the zombie over Cleo's shoulder.

"Watch my bandages," squealed Cleo. "You'll scorch them."

"Excuse me for saving you," snapped Resus, pushing the torch into the zombie's chest. "Now, get behind me!" he yelled as the creature released the mummy and began to bat furiously at the flames.

Luke and Cleo fell into position behind Resus as he kept the zombies at bay with the length of burning wood.

"Brain drain! Brain drain!"

"They're everywhere!" exclaimed Cleo, glancing over the fence to see four more zombies fighting their way out of the neighbor's flower bed.

"How do we get out of here?" asked Luke.

"I think we might have to call on your furry friend," suggested Resus.

Luke sighed. His capacity to change into a werewolf was what had brought his family to Scream Street in the first place. Now he was in the middle of a quest that would enable him to take his parents home, and he wasn't going to jeopardize it by using his powers to attack anyone.

"I won't hurt people," he said quietly.

"You can't hurt them," retorted Resus. "They're dead!"

"No," said Luke. "They're *undead,* and from what I've seen around here, that's a small but vital difference."

"*You* find us a way out, then, Mr. Kind-and-Caring," said Resus.

"Hang on," said Luke. "Can anyone else hear music?"

As they all stopped to listen, the sound of a pounding drumbeat and matching bass line echoed out across Scream Street. "Where's it coming from?" asked Cleo.

"*They* seem to know," said Luke as the zombies suddenly lost interest in the trio and turned to face the source of the music. Slowly they lurched out of the yard, toward Scream Street's Central Square.

"Brain drain! Brain drain!"

"Something strange is going on," said Resus. "We'd better get to the square and find out what."

 9

"I'll meet you there," said Luke. "I'd better make sure my mom and dad are OK first. They'll freak out if any of these zombies turn up in *our* backyard." As he raced off in one direction, across the yards, Resus and Cleo set off in the other.

After a moment's silence, a small voice spoke up. "Who's going to put me back together?" asked Dr. Skully.

# Chapter Two
# The Clue

**Resus and Cleo** skidded to a halt as they arrived in Scream Street. Zombies tottered out of every yard. Cracked hands pushed up through flower beds, and body parts of all descriptions lay scattered about as a vast army of the undead marched to the sound of the same monotonous phrase.

"Brain drain! Brain drain!"

"There are thousands of them," cried Cleo, "and they're all heading for the square!"

"At least that's away from Luke's house," said Resus with relief as he saw that the zombies were lurching in the opposite direction of his friend's retreating figure.

Although Luke had quickly made friends in Scream Street, his parents remained terrified of the world into which they had been thrown. Since arriving in their new home, they had suffered poltergeist attacks, a vampire plague, and an invasion of spiders. Several thousand walking corpses might just push them over the edge.

Resus and Cleo followed the tide of zombies toward the square. One of them reached out to Resus as it staggered past, black drool dripping from its mouth. The vampire ducked under the creature's arms. "Watch out," he warned Cleo. "I think the walk is making them hungry."

"Well, *I've* got nothing to worry about," said Cleo. "My brain is wrapped in waxed paper in the fridge at home."

"But they'll have to crack open your skull to

find that out," Resus noted, grinning as Cleo's expression fell.

The journey was slow going, as the pair could move only at the same shuffling pace as the zombies around them. They craned their necks to get a glimpse of what was drawing the zombies on, but their view was blocked by a sea of decomposing heads. The closer they got to the center of Scream Street, the louder the music became. By the time they reached the main square, the drumbeat and bass line were almost deafening.

Cleo and Resus stared. They were surrounded by thousands of dancing zombies, all lurching in time to the music. Occasionally a cracking sound would ring out, followed by a scream, as one of the more enthusiastic undead snapped a leg bone and fell to the ground.

"This is crazy!" said Cleo.

"It officially freaks *me* out," agreed Resus. Then he caught a glimpse of a booth set up in the corner of the square. A zombie wearing a backward baseball cap stood behind it. "Look!" Resus said. "That's where the music's coming from."

Cleo winced as a boogying zombie staggered

sideways and stepped on her toes. She tried to force her way between two more of them but quickly became jammed. "What do we do now?" she asked. "I can't move."

Resus pulled a pair of sunglasses from his cloak and put them on. "We dance!" he said with a grin.

When Luke finally caught up with Resus and Cleo, he was amazed to find them dancing beside the DJ booth. "Have you two gone insane?"

"It's the fastest way to get anywhere," explained Resus. "Besides, if you dance, they think you're one of them and stop nagging for a taste of your brain."

"Try it," added Cleo.

Luke's face fell. "You surely don't expect me to—"

A nearby zombie in a ragged tuxedo made a grab for him.

"Brain drain! Brain drain!"

Luke began to tap his feet in time to the music and the zombie instantly lost interest. "I feel stupid," he moaned as he flung his arm out in a classic disco pose and, in doing so, slapped a second

 14

zombie in the face. When he pulled his hand back, there was an eyeball stuck to the end of his thumb.

"You'll feel considerably more stupid if one of these guys takes a bite out of your gray matter," warned Resus.

Luke shook his hand violently to rid himself of the rogue eyeball. Several of the zombies around him took this to be a new dance move and copied it. "In that case, I'll get with the beat!"

"How are your mom and dad?" asked Cleo, trying out a complicated twist.

"Shaken, but safe," said Luke, jiggling

awkwardly. "I've locked them in the bathroom until it's safe for them to come out."

"When will that be?" asked Resus.

"I have no idea," admitted Luke. "Although . . . I nearly forgot. I grabbed this on the way back out." He pulled a book from his pocket and spoke to the face embossed on its silver cover. "What's happening, Mr. Skipstone?"

The book was *Skipstone's Tales of Scream Street*. Upon his death many years before, its author, Samuel Skipstone, had cast a spell to merge himself with the pages of his work. This enabled the scholar to continue his research into the street's unusual residents.

The metallic face opened its eyes and looked around. "I'm afraid this is a new experience, even for me," Skipstone replied. "The most recent record I have for a gathering of zombies relates to an occurrence over three hundred years ago, when eight of them turned up with a picnic blanket, a bottle of spinal fluid, and a half-eaten zebra."

"Well, we'd better find out soon," said Luke, hurriedly speeding up his dancing as a drooling zombie glared down at him. "My mom and dad are terrified."

"Then I assume you will also want to know where to find the next founding father's relic?" said Skipstone. With the book's help, Luke had already tracked down three of six artifacts left by Scream Street's first residents. Once he collected them all, he would have the power to open a doorway out of the community and take his parents home.

"Now?" asked Luke. "But there are zombies everywhere!"

"I think you'll find my words strangely appropriate," the author said, smiling.

The trio watched as *Skipstone's Tales of Scream Street* flipped its pages, which were filled with scrawled handwriting and sketched illustrations. It stopped at a short story entitled "Goldifangs and the Three Banshees." The words slowly faded away and were soon replaced with the clue to the next relic's location:

> Once deceased, now living dead,
> trust the creature that you dread.
> Find the zombie, hear him moan,
> make his flesh your very own.

"A zombie's flesh," Luke said with a gasp.

"Well," said Cleo. "We've got plenty to choose from."

"But only one was the first to live in Scream Street," reminded Resus.

Luke stared at the hordes of dancing zombies around them. "How are we ever going to find the right one among this bunch?"

Resus pulled a bottle of beer from his cape and grinned. "We talk to our man on the inside!" As he flipped the top from the beer bottle, a hand shot out of the crowd and grabbed it. It was Doug.

"Cheers, little dude!" The familiar face beamed, taking a long drink.

"Doug, what's going on?" asked Resus.

"Party's going on, my man," replied the zombie, wiggling his hips.

"No, I mean, what's all this about?"

Doug smiled, revealing the maggots crawling around inside his mouth. "It's the greatest zombie rock festival in the world, man."

"Zombie rock festival?" asked Luke.

"Dudes, welcome to Deadstock!"

Cleo gazed around the square. "It's—"

"Totally awesome, I know!" said Doug excitedly. "Me and Turf were psyched when it was relocated here at the last minute." He gestured toward the zombie spinning records. "This here's my main man, Flatboy Skin." Resus tried not to stare as he realized that the zombie was only a couple of millimeters thick—and had tire marks running up the front of his body.

The DJ nodded his wafer-thin head toward them. "Whassup?"

"What are *those* guys doing?" asked Luke, indicating a team of zombies in ragged overalls who were moving wooden boards around.

"They're setting up the stage, little dude," replied Doug. "Ready for our headlining act, Brain Drain."

"Brain Drain!" exclaimed Cleo. "So the zombies weren't after our brains at all."

 19

Doug fixed the trio with a serious stare. "Brain eating is strictly off-limits during Deadstock," he said, adding in a whisper, "although I know a guy who can get you a nice juicy spleen for the right price. . . ."

"But the zombies were grabbing at us!" said Resus.

"It's the spirit of Deadstock, dudes," replied the zombie. "Hug and be hugged! There was a song about it on Brain Drain's second album."

"I almost hate to ask," said Luke, leaning against a tall black speaker, "but who, or what, *are* Brain Drain?"

"Dudes," enthused Doug, "they're only the hottest flesh-metal band in the world! The Drab Four themselves! This is one of their songs playing now: 'Eat Up from the Feet Up.' Vein is such a righteous singer."

Luke, Resus, and Cleo strained to listen to the song's lyrics over the noise of a screeching electric guitar.

*"Biting, chewing, ripping, crunching!"* screamed the singer. "I'm gonna dine on you!"

Luke smiled politely. "It's great."

"It's loud," added Cleo.

"It's *finished*!" growled a voice, and the music suddenly came to a stop. Luke, Resus, and Cleo spun around to discover Sir Otto Sneer, the landlord of Scream Street, behind them at the DJ booth. Clutched in his hand was an electrical plug, and smoke curled up from the noxious cigar clamped between his teeth.

"Deadstock is over!" he roared.

# Chapter Three
# The Meeting

**Gradually the dancing zombies** realized there was no longer any music playing. One by one they turned around to glare at Sir Otto.

"I don't know who told you freaks to come here," bellowed the landlord, "but if you don't leave immediately, I'll have G.H.O.U.L. banish you all to the Underlands!"

Luke shuddered. G.H.O.U.L.—Government

Housing of Unusual Life-forms — was the organization that had sent the Movers to relocate his family to Scream Street. Sir Otto's threat was not one to be taken lightly.

"Whoa," said Doug. "Chill out, dude!"

"Chill out?" roared Sir Otto, throwing the plug to the ground. *"Chill out?"*

A tall, younger man with lank red hair appeared behind the landlord and whispered in his ear, "Uncle Otto . . ."

"*Sir* Otto!"

"Sorry," whispered Dixon, the landlord's nephew. "Sir Uncle Otto, I don't think he really wants you to get chilly. I just think he means you should relax."

Sir Otto's face turned purple. "I'll show them what I do to relax!" Snatching the Brain Drain album from the turntable, he smashed it to the ground.

Doug stared at the broken record in horror. "No way!"

"*That's* what I do to relax," screeched Sir Otto, grabbing another record from the DJ's box. "That, and *this*!" The irate man hurled the record out into the crowd like a Frisbee, where it wedged itself into the soft flesh of a nearby zombie's face.

"Ouch!"

As Sir Otto reached for another record, Flatboy Skin growled. "Petal!" he commanded in a low voice.

Luke was jolted as the wall behind him began to move. It took him a second to realize that it wasn't the speakers he'd been leaning against, but the stomach of a massive zombie dressed all in black.

"Boss?" asked Petal, cracking the bones in his neck menacingly.

The DJ pointed to Sir Otto with a flat hand. The security guard grabbed the landlord's collar with a fist the size of a chair, lifting him clear off the ground. He lurched toward the gates of Sir Otto's mansion, Sneer Hall.

"What are you doing?" shouted the landlord. "PUT ME DOWN THIS MINUTE!"

Dixon ran to catch up with Petal. Tapping the zombie's shoulder, he asked, "Can I get a lift, please?" The huge zombie grunted and swung the thin man over his shoulder. "Thank you!"

"Dixon, you moron," came the muffled voice

of Sir Otto as the security guard carried the two men off. "You're a shapeshifter! Why don't you change into something useful?"

Doug winked at the DJ as he plugged the record player back in. "I think we need to drown out that noise, dude."

Flatboy Skin dropped another record onto the turntable, and within seconds the sound of Brain Drain rang out across the square once more.

"Man, that was bogus," said Doug as the zombies began to dance again. "I hate to think

how these guys would react if Brain Drain didn't appear!"

"Speaking of 'these guys,'" said Luke, "we're trying to find a particular zombie. The first zombie ever to live in Scream Street."

"Tough task, little dude," replied Doug. "If you ask me, you want to speak to the guy who organized this shindig."

"Who is it?" asked Cleo. "Who's in charge?"

Doug pointed a scabby finger toward a shimmering figure supervising the building of the stage. "Our very own neighbor, and president of Moantown Records, Simon Howl!"

More and more zombies poured into Central Square as Luke, Resus, and Cleo danced their way from the DJ booth to the stage. Movement of any kind was becoming increasingly difficult.

"We're getting nowhere fast," said Resus, opening the gate to the nearest house. "Let's go around the outside of the square, through the yards." He led the way across a lawn that was pockmarked with holes. More of the creatures were appearing by the minute.

"Be careful, Cleo," warned Luke as a drooling,

lipless zombie stumbled toward them. "These ones might not know the no-brainer rule yet."

Cleo made a face. "You two haven't got any faith in me, have you?"

"It's not that," said Resus. "But out of the three of us, it's usually you who gets captured, lost, or injured."

"And I suppose I need protecting because I'm a girl, do I?"

"There she goes again." Resus sighed, pushing through the hedge into the next yard. Luke followed, shaking his head.

"I'm not stupid!" Cleo shouted after them. "I know that—"

She suddenly found herself being lifted off her feet. It was the gray zombie with one eye.

"Brain drain! Brain drain!"

"Ow! I know it's in the spirit of Deadstock and all that," shouted Cleo, "but that hurts!" The zombie clutched her to his chest, smothering her face in his diseased skin and muffling her cries for help. Luke and Resus carried on, oblivious.

"*Mmph mm-mpph!*" grunted Cleo, grimacing against the awful stench of the zombie as it carried her along.

"Brain drain! Brain drain!"

Cleo felt her consciousness begin to drift away as the creature clutched her tighter and tighter.

A pale green hand shot up from one of the holes and gripped the zombie's ankle. The monster fell, dropping Cleo to the grass. The mummy staggered to her feet, but before she could run, the same green hand grabbed her leg and pulled her into the hole and underground.

As her eyes grew accustomed to the darkness of the tunnel, Cleo found herself face-to-face with a young zombie: a boy about the same age as herself.

"P-please don't hurt me," stammered Cleo, trying to back away.

The zombie moved into a thin shaft of light that shone down from above. Raising a finger to his cracked lips, he gestured for her to be quiet.

Above them, the ground shook as Cleo's captor stomped around the yard, searching for his lost prize. "Brain drain! Brain drain!"

After a moment the footsteps thudded away.

"You saved me," said Cleo.

The young zombie stared at her. "You're not like the others," he said.

"I'm not a zombie, if that's what you mean," replied the mummy. "My name is Cleo. What's yours?"

The young zombie shrugged unhappily. "I don't know."

"You mean you can't remember who you were before . . ."

"Before I died," finished the zombie. He shook his head. "I woke up inside a coffin, unable to think clearly. The wood was rotten, so I broke through and followed the others up to the surface."

"There's a letter *T* on your jacket," said Cleo, pointing to the embroidered symbol. "Maybe your name starts with a *T*?"

"I don't know," said the young zombie sadly. He reached out and clutched Cleo's hand. "I'm so scared!"

"Of the other zombies?"

The creature nodded. "They all want to tear people apart and eat their brains. I just want to know who I am. I want to remember."

"I could try and help you remember," suggested Cleo.

The zombie looked at her in surprise. "You'd do that?"

"Well, you did save me from being hugged to death," Cleo said with a laugh. "And don't worry about your name," she added, pointing to the zombie's jacket again. "I can call you Tee until we find out what it really is."

"You're kind," Tee said, his green face brightening. "It's been a long time since I met anyone who was kind to me."

Cleo smiled. "I know what it's like to lose your—"

Four hands suddenly reached into the hole and grabbed Cleo, hauling her out of the tunnel. "We can't leave you alone for two minutes, can we?" said Luke.

"That's the last you'll see of *that* diseased monster," said Resus, laughing, kicking a mound of dirt into the hole and collapsing the tunnel over Tee.

The zombie stretched his hand toward Cleo. "Please . . ." he begged as the soil covered his terrified face and he was lost from view.

"No!" shouted Cleo. "Stop!" She pulled free of Luke's grip and dropped to her knees, digging frantically with her hands.

"You don't have to prove anything by going back down there," said Luke.

"He saved me!" snapped Cleo.

"Yes," Resus said, smirking. "I suppose I did."

"Not *you*," roared Cleo. "That zombie! One of the bigger ones grabbed me, and the one in the tunnel saved me from him!"

"One zombie saved you from another zombie?" asked Luke. "He probably just wanted your brain for himself."

"He wanted nothing of the sort," shouted Cleo. "He wanted my help."

"He wants your lungs for lunch, more likely," said Resus.

"He's not like the others," insisted Cleo. "He's

31

lost and he's frightened! Now, help me get him out of this hole."

Reluctantly, Resus dropped to the ground and joined in with the digging. Luke grabbed a nearby garden rake and stood guard, knocking any curious zombies to one side. After a few minutes, the tunnel became visible. Cleo jumped down into it and peered through the darkness.

Tee was gone.

**Resus hurried** after Cleo as she stormed through the hedge into the next yard. "I'm sorry," he said. "We didn't know that zombie was trying to help you."

"You just can't stand that someone my own age wanted to talk to me, can you!" exclaimed Cleo.

"Your own age?" scoffed Resus. "Unless he was entombed in a pyramid about six thousand years ago, I doubt he's anywhere near your age."

"You're just jealous because he's a *real* zombie," said Cleo.

"What do you mean by that?" demanded Resus, although he knew exactly what Cleo was referring to. He was something of a genetic oddity in his family: a normal child born to vampire parents. He hated the taste of blood, could stay outside in the daylight, and was reduced to wearing clip-on fangs.

Cleo spun and pushed her face closer to Resus's. "Let's just say *he* doesn't feel the need to dye his hair black."

"That's not fair!" protested Resus. "I only use the stuff so I won't be an embarrassment to my family."

"Who says that hair dye stops that from happening?"

"Sorry to break up this touching moment," said Luke as they reached the last yard, leading back into the square, "but could we please save it for when we're not overrun with zombies?"

The trio soon found themselves next to the vast stage that the overall-clad zombies had been building.

"Excuse me," Cleo asked the nearest one. "We're looking for Simon How—"

She jumped as the phantom materialized in front of her.

"Well, looky here," the ghost said with a

smile, running a hand through his wildly teased hair. "We got ourselves some flesh-metal music fans!"

"Actually, Mr. Howl," said Resus, "we know you're—"

"President of Moantown Records!" interrupted the spirit, pressing a translucent business card into Resus's palm. "And, of course, the man who brought Deadstock to Scream Street."

"This is your doing?" asked Luke. "My parents are scared out of their minds!"

"So they should be," said Howl, beaming. "It's not every day a top zombie band like Brain Drain plays in your own backyard."

"You're missing the point," said Resus. "We're looking for one zombie in particular."

"As am I!" interrupted a female voice. Luke looked up to see Eefa Everwell, the witch who ran Scream Street's general store, pushing her way through the crowds. The witch's enchantment charm caused every zombie she passed to stop and stare at her utter beauty.

"Everwell's Emporium has been broken into," she announced.

"What makes you think it was one of the zombies?" asked Simon Howl.

"I'd popped home for a moment," said Eefa, producing a crystal ball from beneath her robes, "but my security spell caught the culprit red-handed!" An image began to glow inside the glass sphere. Cleo nudged Luke to stop him from gaping at the witch's beauty, and they all crowded around to watch.

Inside the globe, a tall zombie with lank red hair smashed into the emporium through the door from the stockroom and proceeded to demolish the shop. He knocked over shelves, smashed display stands, and tore up paperwork.

"Did he take much?" Cleo asked the witch.

"Just a few basic spell ingredients, from what I can tell," replied Eefa. "But everything's in such a mess, I don't really know what's there and what isn't." She rounded on the president of Moantown Records. "I kept the emporium open today for Deadstock," said Eefa, "because you, Simon, assured me there would be no trouble!"

"Now, hold on a minute," protested the phantom. "I cannot be held responsible for the actions of every zombie who's come to see their favorite band."

"Perhaps not," said Eefa, "but you *can* reimburse me for the damage."

"Reimburse you?" barked Howl.

"Excuse me, Mr. Howl," said Luke. "I know this isn't the best time, but I need to ask you—"

"For some backstage passes, I know," interjected the ghost, pulling three laminated cards from his clipboard. "There you go, kids—now run along and let Miss Everwell and I sort out this problem."

Luke found a pass thrust at him and a hand the size of a door at his back, pushing him toward a black silk tent set up at the rear of the stage.

"No," he objected, "you don't understand . . ."

"Forget it," said Resus. "You've got more chance of escaping from the Underlands than you have of getting a straight answer there!"

"Sir Otto mentioned the Underlands earlier," said Luke. "What are they?"

Cleo shivered. "Something not to be talked about, if you ask me."

"The Underlands is another realm," explained Resus. "A terrifying place that saps your spirit

and keeps you in a constant state of doom and despair."

"Sounds like a great place for a vacation!"

"Don't believe it," said Resus, missing Luke's joke. "The Underlands is where G.H.O.U.L. sends all the really nasty beings—creatures that can't be trusted to live among the likes of us without causing carnage."

"I wouldn't have thought Scream Street had that many bad characters to begin with," commented Luke.

"They come from G.H.O.U.L. communities all over the world," explained Resus.

Luke looked amazed. "You mean there are other places like Scream Street?"

"In just about every country," said Cleo. "My dad and I lived in a town in Australia before we were moved here."

"And *we* were supposed to be performing in Scandinavia today," snarled a voice. "Not this provincial dump!"

Luke, Resus, and Cleo turned toward the voice, which had come from the black tent. A green face wearing small black sunglasses peered through a gap in the material.

"Are you talking to us?" asked Resus, stepping toward the tent.

"Stay right where you are," ordered the face.

"It's OK," said Cleo. "We're friends of Mr. Howl's. He gave us backstage passes."

"I don't care if he gave you Frankenstein's phone number," growled the figure. "I told you to stay back!"

"How dare—" began Resus.

Luke nudged his friend in the ribs. "Are you with the band?" he asked.

The figure stepped out from the confines of the tent. He was tall and slim, with tattoos covering almost every inch of his green skin. Luke was amazed to see that the zombie wasn't wearing sunglasses after all—his eyes were just jet black.

"I'm not *with* the band," snarled the figure. "I *am* the band!"

"But Doug told us that Brain Drain had four members," said Cleo.

The zombie smoothed back his slicked black hair. "Even a legend like Vein needs musicians behind him."

"*You're* Vein?" asked Resus. "You're the lead singer!"

"You catch on quick," drawled the slim zombie, "for a vampire."

"You take that back!" protested Resus. "Or I'll—"

Luke interrupted. "Did you say you were supposed to be performing in Scandinavia today?"

"Aren't *you* clever for remembering."

"Deadstock wasn't supposed to be in Scream Street, then?" asked Cleo, trying her best to ignore the singer's sarcasm.

"The venue was changed at the last minute due to an outbreak of hoof-and-mouth disease among the Swedish demons," grumbled Vein. "Next thing I know, G.H.O.U.L.'s opened a Hex Hatch and we're here."

Cleo shrugged. "So, what's the problem?"

"I wouldn't choose to play hide-and-seek in a dump like this, let alone a rock concert."

"Do you mind?" snapped Resus. "This is our home."

Vein chuckled nastily. "It suits you."

Luke struggled to hold Resus back. "How did the zombies know?"

"How did the zombies know what?" asked Vein, sounding bored.

"How did the zombies know that the venue had been changed?"

Vein jerked a thumb back in the direction of the tent. "Twonk, our drummer, runs the Brain Drain fan club. He must have contacted everyone."

Luke stared thoughtfully at the slim opening in the black silk. "There's a list!" he exclaimed. "We don't need Simon Howl; the drummer's got a list of every zombie here. We can find our zombie

that way!" He took a step toward the tent, but
Vein slapped a hand on Luke's shoulder.

"You are not to disturb anyone in my band
before we perform," he warned. As he spoke,
three other zombies came out of the tent carrying musical instruments and climbed up onto the
stage.

"You don't understand," said Luke. "I need
to find a particular zombie."

Vein leaped up onto the stage and glared
down at the trio. "It's bad enough having to play
a dive like Scream Street without kids like you
hanging around as well!"

"And what would *you* know about Scream
Street?" Resus asked hotly.

"I used to live here," said Vein over his shoulder as he strode off after the rest of the band.
"In fact, I believe I was the first zombie ever to
do so."

# Chapter Five
# The Spell

**Luke, Resus, and Cleo** ran around to the front of the stage. "*He's* one of Scream Street's founding fathers?" spluttered Resus.

"But, he's horrible!" said Cleo.

"I guess you don't have to be pleasant to be

the first of your kind to live somewhere," said Luke.

"We should look on the bright side," said Resus. "At least we don't have to search through the drummer's fan club list now."

"That's true," agreed Luke, "but we *do* have to ask Vein for his relic."

An eerie hush filled the square as Simon Howl materialized before the microphone at the front of the stage. "Lamies and gentlemoans," he announced. "Today is the happiest day of your deaths. The greatest rock group ever to taste flesh has arrived here—yes, *here*—in Scream Street. It's . . . Brain Drain!"

The audience went wild, cheering, applauding, and screaming.

"Looks like we'll have to watch the show first," said Cleo.

Simon Howl continued. "On drums, the monster who puts the beat in *deadbeat*—Twonk!" The spotlight fell on a jolly, round-faced zombie clutching a pair of arm bones. He sat at a drum kit covered with stretched human skin and began to pound out a powerful rhythm.

"On bass," continued Howl, "it's the quiet

one—although that could be because his lips fell off during their last tour—Porridge!" The female zombies in the audience screamed as a tall, thin creature appeared in the lights, his long green hair flopping down over his eyes. Porridge plugged in a bass guitar made from a leg with tendons for strings, and joined in with the drums.

"Next," said Simon Howl, "on lead guitar, the sultry siren who makes those strings sing—Jazpants!" This time it was the male monsters' turn to go crazy as a female zombie dashed out onto the stage clutching a guitar formed out of a human spine, on which she played a wild solo. Cleo nudged Luke and pointed to the guitarist's hands. Jazpants had eight fingers on each hand, the extra digits having been stitched on beside her own.

"And finally," announced Simon Howl as the musicians continued to play, "the greatest super-star ever to crawl out of a coffin. The viscount of vocals himself! Give it up for the one, the only—Vein!"

The lead singer of Brain Drain sauntered casually onto the stage to deafening applause and cheers. Several of the zombies near the front of the crowd fainted from excitement, crumpling to the ground.

Vein took the microphone from Howl, paused theatrically, driving the crowd insane, and began to sing in a deep, gravelly voice.

*"If I rip the heart right from your chest,*
*They'll take me away; cardiac arrest. . . ."*

Simon Howl shimmered into existence beside Luke, Resus, and Cleo. "What did I tell you?" he shouted over the noise of the band. "Aren't they great?"

"Wonderful!" yelled Resus, twisting the corners of his cape and pushing them into his ears.

Vein sang to the entranced crowd:

*"I'll let your blood flow like a river,*
*Mop it all up with your juicy liver."*

"Catchy lyrics," said Luke.

"It's called 'Zombie Feasting Time,'" shouted Simon Howl. "It was written by one of the band's fans and delivered anonymously to Vein this morning."

"Composed by the decomposed. How appropriate!"

Cleo scanned the audience of madly dancing zombies. Heads, arms, and torsos flew into the air as the creatures clashed against one another in the musical mêlée. Suddenly she spotted a familiar face. "Tee!" she screamed, racing into the crowd.

Resus grabbed Luke's arm. "Come on!" he shouted.

The trio pushed their way through the heavy crowd, searching for the young zombie. "Tee!" yelled Cleo, the pumping music almost completely drowning out her voice. Resus pulled a tennis racket from his cloak and began to bat dancing monsters out of their way.

"Are you OK?" Cleo asked as they reached Tee.

The young zombie shook his head, dazed. "I don't know what's happening."

"It's OK," said Resus. "We've only got the vaguest idea ourselves!"

"Let's get out of here," said Luke. "We can talk to Vein after the show."

Resus began to create a pathway through the zombies by batting at them with the tennis racket. Body parts bounced around.

Cleo grabbed Tee's hand and began to steer him through the crowd, with Luke bringing up the rear. "Don't worry," she assured the zombie. "We'll be out of here soon."

Suddenly one of the zombies who had found himself on the wrong end of Resus's racket spun around and grabbed Luke's shoulder, digging its nails in deep.

 49

Luke yelled in pain. "What did you do that f—" He staggered as a familiar feeling began to wash over him. "Cleo . . ." he managed to croak before his mind was wrapped in darkness.

"Resus," called the mummy. "Luke's transforming!"

The bones in Luke's arms cracked noisily as they stretched, muscles growing and wrapping themselves around the stronger limbs. Long yellow talons burst from the ends of his fingers.

This was one of the many partial transformations Luke had experienced since moving to Scream Street, where only one part of his body changed into that of a werewolf. He was often not fully in control over what would change: this time his arms rippled with brown fur and ended in powerful claws.

The werewolf inside Luke glared up at the zombie still gripping his shoulder. Lashing out with his paws, he sliced at the creature's chest, sending it crashing to the ground.

Having seen one of their own injured, the other zombies around the part-werewolf pounced. Luke punched out again and again, desperate to keep his attackers at bay. Resus thrust the racket back into his cloak and pulled out the flaming torch.

"Get away from him!" he shouted, jabbing it into the crowd as Brain Drain's music continued to pound across the square.

The zombies stepped back, spooked by the flame. Cleo and Tee hurried to Resus's side as he twisted from left to right, trying to keep the monsters back, and the group found itself in a circle of angry, snarling zombies.

"OK," said Cleo slowly. "Any idea what we do now?"

*"Chewing on you, you're tasting good,*
*Gnawing your bones and—"*

Suddenly a piercing scream rang out through the sound system, and all eyes turned toward the stage. Vein's feet were wrapped in a swirling green mist that quickly rose up his body until, with a flash, the singer disappeared.

"What on earth?" Resus asked, amazed.

As the audience watched, another cloud of green gas appeared and wrapped around Jazpants, her instrument clattering to the floor as she vanished.

The bass guitarist was next to be swallowed

up by the vapor. Porridge gurgled a yell as the mist enveloped him.

Twonk, the only member of Brain Drain left on the stage, stopped playing as the gas began to hiss around his feet. The drummer jumped up and leaped from the stage in an effort to escape, but the green cloud was around him within seconds; he disappeared before he hit the ground.

The zombie crowd stared in silence as a figure strode out onto the stage where their heroes had so recently stood. A large man puffed hard on a noxious cigar.

"I have two things to say," Sir Otto Sneer roared into the microphone. "One: never, *ever* mess with me. And two: meet the composer of Brain Drain's latest hit!"

Simon Howl materialized beside the landlord. "*You* wrote 'Zombie Feasting Time'?"

"Not bad for a first try, is it?" Sir Otto said with a grin. "I had a bit of a problem finding a rhyme for kidney, but I got there in the end."

"What happened to the band?" demanded Howl.

"Let's just say there was magic in the music," crowed Sir Otto as a zombie with lank red hair

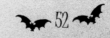

climbed onto the stage and stood beside him.

"That's the zombie who raided the emporium," hissed Resus.

The red-haired zombie's skin began to ripple and clear of its scabs as his body twisted back to its original shape. Fully transformed, the thin figure waved cheerily to the crowd from his uncle's side. "Coo-ee!"

"It's Dixon!" said Cleo. "He shapeshifted into a zombie to break into Everwell's!" Beside her, Luke groaned as his claws transformed back into human hands.

All across the square, zombies began to complain. "Brain Drain!" shouted one of the creatures. Those around it joined in with the chant. "Brain Drain!"

Simon Howl raised a hand to silence them. "Where *is* Brain Drain?"

The landlord sucked hard on his cigar. "They've set off on a never-ending tour," he said, his voice echoing through the speaker system so no one could fail to hear his words. "To the Underlands."

At the mention of this, a shocked hush fell across the crowd, then the zombies began to lurch forward, pressing against the stage. Sir Otto remained unmoved by the moans and growls around him.

"If you freaks ever want to see Brain Drain again," he roared, pointing directly at Luke, "bring me *that* werewolf!"

# Chapter Six
# The Underlands

**Two huge zombies** pinned Luke's now human arms firmly behind his back as he was lifted onto the stage to face Sir Otto. Resus, Cleo, and Tee were bundled up to stand with their friend.

"What do you want?" growled Luke.

"I would have thought that was obvious," Sir Otto said with a sneer. "I'll take *Skipstone's*

*Tales of Scream Street,* for a start, then there are the relics . . ."

Luke glared through the cloud of cigar smoke into the landlord's greedy eyes. Sir Otto would use the combined power of the founding fathers' relics to make the lives of Scream Street's residents as miserable as possible.

"And what if I decide not to give them to you?" asked Luke.

"Then I toss you to this angry mob, and they take out their disappointment over the end of Deadstock on you," Sir Otto said with a smile. "Once the zombies have finished plundering your corpses, I'll help myself to Skipstone's book anyway."

Luke glanced down at the furious zombies pressing against the front of the stage. One of them had a broken neck, its top vertebra jutting through a gash at the back of its head. It hissed angrily.

Luke fixed his eyes on Sir Otto. "I don't think you've got the *backbone*."

Resus's eyes widened. "Er, Luke . . ." he said. "What are you doing?"

"He's *spine*less," replied Luke. "Whatever he takes, we'll get it *back*."

"Luke!" hissed Resus. "What are you . . .?"

"Make no *bones* about it," added Luke, as slowly and as clearly as he could. "He'll get it in the *neck*."

"What are you talking about?" demanded Resus.

Cleo squealed in frustration. "Keep it up!" she shouted. Reaching down, she grabbed the hissing zombie's exposed white backbone and pulled. With a sickening squelch, the monster's spine slid out of its body. There was a *pfft!* and the zombie crumpled to the ground.

Swinging the spine around, Cleo caught Sir Otto full in the face. The landlord's cigar was thrust into his mouth, burning the tender skin at the back of his throat. He scrabbled around, gesturing wildly for someone to slap his back.

Meanwhile, the zombies holding Luke were distracted long enough for him to wriggle out of their grasp. He ran to the back of the stage, pushing over a wall of speakers to allow himself, Cleo, Resus, and Tee to jump safely to the ground.

The audience swarmed over the stage after them.

"What now?" asked Resus as the four of them ran from the charging zombies.

"The only thing we can do," said Luke. "We go to the Underlands!"

Resus lifted the metal grate a few inches and peered out cautiously. A full-scale zombie riot was in progress. Luke, Resus, Cleo, and Tee had managed to outrun the creatures, ducking into a drain at the back of Sneer Hall. The furious monsters, unable to find the people they considered responsible for the disappearance of Brain Drain, had turned their frustrations on Scream Street itself.

They lurched along the streets, smashing windows, uprooting lampposts, and demolishing fences. The terrified residents hastily barricaded themselves into their homes.

Resus dropped the drain cover and slumped back into the hole. "You know we're going to get the blame for this," he said.

"But it was Sneer's fault," said Cleo. "He's the one who wrote that stupid song and fired the band off to who knows where!"

Resus grinned wryly. "Talk about one-hit Underlands."

"I still don't get it," admitted Luke. "How can singing a song cause you to vanish in a puff of smoke?"

"It must have been the spell ingredients Dixon stole from Everwell's," said Resus. "If Sir Otto mixed them together as he wrote the song, playing and singing it could well be the key to releasing the spell's effects. Sort of like a password."

"We could do with something like that to get us out of this drain," groaned Luke, struggling to make himself comfortable against the damp wall.

"And it stinks down here," said Tee.

"Well, feel free to walk away anytime," snorted Resus.

"We aren't leaving Tee to the mercy of those monsters," said Cleo defensively, glaring at the vampire in the darkness.

"He's *one* of those monsters!" countered Resus.

"Resus Negative," snapped Cleo, "I would have thought that you, of all people, would appreciate that you shouldn't judge a person by their appearance."

"If you're going to start on about me not being a real vampire again—"

"Nobody's starting anything," Luke interrupted hurriedly. "We've got a problem, and the only way to solve it is to go to this Underlands place and get Brain Drain back up here to continue playing."

"You're crazy," said Resus. "No one goes to the Underlands on purpose!"

"Well, if we've got any hope of collecting the next relic from Vein," said Luke, "I guess we're going to have to be the first."

"You don't get it. We *can't* go to the Underlands," said Resus. "The only creatures who even vaguely know how to get there are zombies, and as they're all currently out for our blood, we haven't got one to tunnel us there."

Tee cleared his throat. "Actually," he said, "you have."

Resus produced a jar of glowworms from his cloak and used their dim light to check the time. "That's two hours we've been down here," he moaned, "and we're no closer to the Underlands than when we started!"

"You don't know that," said Cleo, collecting up the soil produced by Tee as he dug deeper into the ground. She in turn passed the dirt back to Luke, who used it to fill in the rear of the tunnel. "We could be almost there."

"Nonsense!" scoffed Resus. "I doubt we've traveled more than two or three yards. It'll take days at this rate."

Luke wiped the sweat from his face with a muddy hand. Tunneling under Scream Street was hard enough without Resus and Cleo arguing all the way. "We don't know how far or how deep we've gone," he said patiently. "I suggest we trust Tee's instincts for the time being."

"Instincts?" Resus said with a laugh, flinging his hands out. "He's simply digging in the general direction of down. You don't need zombie instincts to tell you that!"

"Stop waving about," said Luke. "We'll be down here a lot longer if you collapse the tunnel and bury us alive."

Ignoring him, Resus continued to rant. "All I'm saying is that we'll need to dig deeper than the sewer if we hope to get anywhere at all." The vampire punched his fist down to emphasize his

point, and as he did so, his arm smashed through the floor of the tunnel and opened up a hole. Before he could even cry out in shock, the vampire had fallen through it into nothingness.

Luke lunged forward and grabbed his friend's wrist as he slipped through the gap.

"Don't let go!" Resus shouted in panic, his voice echoing around the tunnel above. Risking a glance down, he discovered that he was dangling high above the ground in what looked like another world. The sky was a deep, pulsing red, and Luke's arm appeared to be clutching his own through a bank of swirling plum-colored clouds.

Luke, Cleo, and Tee dragged Resus back through the hole. The vampire struggled to catch his breath. "The Underlands." He gasped. "We're here!"

"All I can see is some kind of purple mist," said Cleo, peering through the hole.

"Trust me, it's down there," said Resus. "A *long* way down there."

"But we've only traveled a few yards," said Luke. "You said so yourself."

Resus shrugged. "I don't know how it's happened, but we're definitely not beneath Scream Street anymore."

"I believe I can shed a little light on your situation," came a muffled voice. Luke pulled *Skipstone's Tales of Scream Street* from his pocket and propped it up against the wall of the tunnel. The book's author was bathed in the mysterious purple light from below. "You appear to have tapped into one of the Hex Hatches put in place by G.H.O.U.L. for the zombies to reach Deadstock."

"Hex Hatches?" asked Luke.

"The Movers are required to relocate families

over considerable distances in a short period of time," explained Skipstone. "A Hex Hatch allows them to travel from one G.H.O.U.L. location to another with ease. Did you not hear the band's singer say they had passed through one to get to Scream Street this morning?"

"So we've been magically transported here, like Brain Drain?" asked Cleo.

"It would be more correct to say you have stumbled upon a magical shortcut," explained Skipstone. "But the end result is much the same."

"This is all very interesting," said Resus, "but it doesn't help us to get down there. We're up at cloud level and I, for one, don't care for a free fall."

"Have you got any rope in your cloak?" asked Luke.

"A bit, maybe, but nothing long enough."

Cleo sighed and began to unwrap the bandages from around her waist. "Leave it to the girl to save the day, yet again."

# Chapter Seven
# The Unicorn

**Luke winced** as he was lowered from the crimson sky on the end of a string of knotted bandages. He tried not to look down, but the view above didn't help much either. The top of the makeshift rope simply disappeared into the churning purple clouds.

"I'm almost there," he called. Unseen in the hole above, Resus was slowly feeding out the rope, controlling his friend's descent.

Finally Luke's feet met the blackened earth below, and he allowed himself to breathe. He turned to Tee as the rope was whisked back up into the air once again. "Where's Cleo?"

"Over here," shouted the mummy from behind a nearby dead tree. "And I'm not coming out until I get my bandages back."

Resus landed beside Luke and tugged at the rope, which detached itself from the tunnel above and fell to the ground. "Simple slipknot," said the vampire, beaming, as he tossed the bundle of bandages behind Cleo's tree.

Luke surveyed the landscape around them. A desert of rough black sand spread out for miles in every direction beneath the bloodred sky. The air felt as though a thunderstorm was approaching.

"Well," said Resus, "*this* is pleasant."

Luke spun to face him. "You didn't have to come with me."

"Oh, yes, I did," replied the vampire. "You'd still be stuck up in the clouds without my help."

"Actually," interrupted Tee, "it was Cleo who got us down."

"You can keep quiet, zombie boy," snapped Resus. "I don't even know why you're here."

"He's here because *I* want him to be here," barked Cleo as she appeared from behind the tree, fully bandaged.

"And of course we have to do what the mummy says, don't we," Luke grunted.

"I've had just about enough—"

Resus raised his hands. "Stop!" he shouted. "This isn't really us arguing."

"Sounds like it to me," retorted Luke.

Resus shook his head. "It's this place. It's sapping our positive energy and aggravating us. We have to try to ignore it."

"That's easy for you to say," grumbled Cleo, brushing black sand from her legs. "'This place' isn't getting inside your bandages." She turned and tripped over something sticking up from the ground, then glared down at it.

"Ouch! That wasn't funny," said the object, causing Cleo to jump in fright. Jutting out of the sand was the head of Brain Drain's drummer, Twonk.

Luke and Resus exchanged a glance, then dropped to their

knees and began to drag sand away from the drummer. "How did you manage to get buried like this?" asked the vampire.

"It's a funny thing," said Twonk. "One minute I was jumping off the stage, and the next I was falling through those purple clowns!"

"Do you mean purple *clouds*?" asked Luke.

"Oh, yeah!" said the zombie with a grin.

Eventually Twonk's shoulders became visible. "OK," said Resus, "we're going to try to pull you out now. How well are your arms stitched on?"

"They're my originals," said Twonk proudly. "Never been detached."

"Let's just hope they stay that way," said Resus. "On three. One . . . two . . . three!" The boys heaved, and after a moment the drummer popped out of the ground.

"That's great," said Twonk, beaming and clambering to his feet. "I could have been stuck there for centurions!"

"I think you mean *centuries*," said Luke.

"Oh, yeah!"

\* \* \*

". . . but the funny thing was, I'd already lost my drumstinks!" Twonk giggled as he finished his twenty-fifth unfunny story in a row.

"Drum*sticks*," growled Luke. "They're called drum*sticks*!"

"Oh, yeah!"

"My feet ache," moaned Tee.

"So do my ears," grumbled Resus, glancing at Twonk. "I don't think he's taken a breath since we found him." The group had been walking for hours but had seen nothing but the same barren landscape, dotted with dead trees. There had certainly been no sign of any other members of Brain Drain.

"A funny thing about breath—" began Twonk.

"I think we'll have to spend the night here," Luke interrupted before the zombie drummer could finish.

"Spend the night?" demanded Resus. "No one said anything about spending the night! My mom and dad will be expecting me home."

"I think they'll have enough to worry about, with the zombie riot and all," said Luke. "I don't

want to stay here any longer than we have to either!"

Resus glared at him. "You're only grumpy because of all the negative energy flying around."

"If you don't stop going on about negative energy . . ."

"It's a funny thing," began Twonk.

"SHUT UP!" shouted Luke and Resus together.

"The problem is, we don't know where the next member of Brain Drain will be," said Cleo. "We need to cover more ground."

"And how do you suggest we do that, brainy-bandages?" asked Resus.

"Simple," said Cleo, sticking her tongue out at him. "We ride." The mummy headed toward a gap in the trees, where she had spied a glowing silver unicorn. Its long spiral horn glittered in the red light of the sky as it stood watching them.

"Cleo, stop right there," said Resus.

"What's the matter?" asked the mummy. "It's just a unicorn."

"A unicorn in the Underlands!" Resus reminded her. "Creatures are only sent here because they're nasty. *Really* nasty!"

"Nonsense," scoffed Cleo, creeping up to the silver beast and running a hand over its shimmering coat. "You're just trying to spoil things again. How can something this beautiful be nasty?"

"Is it me," said Resus to Luke, "or can you feel the phrase 'I told you so' heading toward us?"

"Resus might be right," said Luke. "Better to leave it alone."

"You really are a pair of cowards," mocked Cleo. She reached up to stroke the unicorn on its nose. The animal blew twinkling air from its nostrils and lowered its head so that Cleo could pull herself up onto its back.

"See?" said the mummy. "No problem at all!"

"Be careful . . ."

"Leave her to it," grumbled Luke, turning away. "If she gets hurt, it's her own fault."

"I can't leave her to it," snapped Resus. "That's a horse with a built-in weapon!"

"You mean this silly thing?" asked Cleo, reaching forward to caress the unicorn's horn. "This is just for show, isn't it, boy?"

The unicorn blew another blast of air from its nose, but this time its breath glittered black. Then the creature's eyes melted from silver to red, and

with a deafening whinny, it tossed Cleo high into the air. The beast raised itself up on its back legs and impaled the falling mummy on its pointed horn. Cleo screamed in agony.

"Told you so!" yelled Luke and Resus together as the unicorn took off at a gallop. The three boys and Twonk gave chase across the dead, blackened plain.

"It went through her stomach," shouted Tee. "She can't survive that!"

"She's a mummy," yelled Resus. "Her stomach's in the fridge at home, along with all her

other organs. She'll hurt after this, but she'll live."

"*If* we can catch her," bellowed Luke. "The unicorn's a lot faster than us!"

"I've got an idea," said Resus, dragging a length of rope from his cloak and tying a slipknot in the end as they ran. "But we're only going to get one shot at this," he warned.

Spinning the rope around his head like a cowboy's lasso, Resus tossed the noose toward the retreating beast. It fell against the unicorn's horn and dropped away.

"I missed!" he shouted in frustration.

"Not necessarily," called Tee as the rope slid backward over the creature's tail. He took the end from Resus's hand and yanked hard. The slipknot tightened around the thick hair and the unicorn skidded to a halt.

"There," Tee said, beaming. "That'll be a tale to tell everyone back—"

His breath was knocked from him as the unicorn galloped away again, eyes blazing and foam dripping from its mouth.

Tee was dragged roughly over the sand. His palms burned as the rope threatened to slip

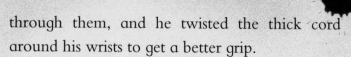

through them, and he twisted the thick cord around his wrists to get a better grip.

Resus, Luke, and Twonk threw themselves at Tee's feet, grabbing his ankles to add their weight. Eventually the unicorn was dragged to a stop, shaking its head angrily. This dislodged Cleo from its horn, and the mummy landed with a crash among a clump of dead bushes.

The boys released the rope and raced over to Cleo as the unicorn galloped off into the distance. She opened her eyes and stared up at them. "That *really* hurt," she groaned.

"I'm not surprised," said Twonk. "You were imposed on its horn!"

"*Impaled,*" snapped Luke, correcting him.

"Oh, yeah!"

"I warned you to stay away from that thing," yelled Resus, hugging Cleo. "Anything could have happened!"

She forced a smile. "I wasn't worried," she said. "I had you to save me."

"Actually," said Luke, "you can thank Tee for that one."

"You did well," admitted Resus, patting the beaming zombie on the shoulder. "Why don't you and Twonk go and find us some firewood? It looks like we'll be spending the night here after all."

As Tee and Twonk lumbered off in search of kindling, Resus turned to Luke with a grin. "If nothing else, it'll be quiet for a while."

Just then, a tortured scream rang out, and the trio turned to see Brain Drain's guitarist, Jazpants, racing across the plain toward them, beating at herself frantically with her eight-fingered hands.

"Me and my big mouth," said the vampire, sighing.

# Chapter Eight
# The Pixies

As **Jazpants** came closer, Luke could see that she was swatting at some strange creatures flying around her. "What are they?" he asked. "Wasps?"

"No such luck," replied Resus, pulling his cloak up over his head. "They're pixies!"

"Pixies?" mocked Luke. "I thought they were

supposed to be cute little — *Ow!*" One of the creatures had zoomed straight for Luke's head, biting his ear and drawing blood.

"They're like flying piranha fish," shouted Resus from under his cape. "They'll attack anything even remotely living!"

Luke yelped as another pixie took a bite at his nose. Jazpants collapsed at his feet, panting and rubbing at the dozens of bites that already covered her.

"What do we do?" shouted Luke as the creatures continued to nip them.

Resus produced a cloth sack. "If we can get them in here, we should be OK."

"You expect me to chase these things around with a bag?"

"No," said Resus, pulling his cape to one side to reveal the tennis racket he had been using earlier. "I expect you to catch them as I serve!" Swinging the racket, he slammed it into the nearest pixie, catapulting the screaming imp directly toward his friend.

Luke opened the bag and the pixie flew inside. "Fifteen–love!" he said with a grin while clamping the sack firmly closed.

For the next twenty minutes, Resus and Luke batted and volleyed the pixies until they'd caught them all. "Game, set, and match," said the vampire, his face beaming.

Cleo forced herself up onto her elbows. "Can you two keep it down?" she asked. "I'm trying to get some rest here."

"Sorry." Resus grinned. "I guess we were making a bit of a racket!"

". . . and the funny thing was, we should have been dancing a tangle," said Twonk.

*"Tango!"* shouted Luke, Resus, Cleo, Tee, and Jazpants together.

"Oh, yeah!"

"Is he always like this?" asked Resus.

Jazpants clutched her ears and ripped them off her head. "I had these made detachable because I have to sit next to him in the van so often."

Luke tossed more wood onto the fire. Twonk and Tee had done well, and the group now had a large pile of deadwood to keep them going. Meanwhile, the sky above had darkened to a deep burgundy, making the Underlands look gloomier than ever.

  78

"How long have you known Vein?" asked Luke as Jazpants stuck her ears back in place.

"Not that long," replied the zombie. "We had a female singer when the band first got together, but she fell apart."

"She couldn't cope with the fame?" asked Cleo.

"No," replied Jazpants. "She literally fell apart—during one of our shows. There were pieces of her everywhere. It's her backbone that I use for my guitar now."

"And then Vein joined the band?" said Resus.

Jazpants nodded. "He took over, started ordering everyone around, and soon we were relegated to little more than *back*up musicians."

Twonk stared sadly into the fire. "That wasn't funny."

"Still," said Jazpants, "that's all in the past now. I doubt Brain Drain will ever play together again."

"We'll find a way to get you out of here," said Luke—adding, more to himself than anyone else, "we have to."

The group fell silent, watching the flames

crackle gently in the fire. After a while, Jazpants began to sing softly, *"I'll bite your spleen and sip your bile . . ."*

Resus pointed at her hands. "Look!"

"What?" asked Luke.

"Sing that again," said Resus. "That line from 'Zombie Feasting Time.'"

"The song Sir Otto wrote?" said Cleo. Resus nodded.

Jazpants took a deep breath and sang once more.

*"I'll bite your spleen and sip your bile,*
*Chew your kidneys for a while. . . ."*

"There!" said Resus excitedly. Wisps of green smoke were bubbling around Jazpants's sixteen fingers. "I think we've just found a way to get you home."

In the orange glow of the fire, Twonk sat behind an assortment of pots and pans from Resus's cape, with two pieces of firewood in his hands to serve as drumsticks.

Beside him, Jazpants readied herself to strum on the trusty tennis racket. "Are you sure this is going to work?" she asked.

"When you sang those lines from 'Zombie Feasting Time,' the green smoke appeared again," insisted Resus. "If we can trick the spell into thinking you're performing the song down here, it might just work in reverse and send you back to Scream Street."

"Or," suggested Luke, "they could wind up several miles underground."

Resus frowned at him. "Let's hope for the best, eh?"

"It's not funny making me play drums on cooking untenables," complained Twonk.

"They're *utensils,*" said Resus through gritted teeth, "and if you want to get out of here, you'll just have to put up with it."

The vampire stood before the two musicians and raised his hands like a conductor. "OK. . . . One, two, three, four!"

Twonk played out a beat on the pots and pans while Jazpants's extra fingers plucked at the taut strings of the tennis racket.

"It's not working," said Luke after a few moments.

"It might be because no one's singing the lyrics," said Resus.

 81

"Don't look at me," said Jazpants. "I can only remember that one line."

"And I've never been any good at limits," added Twonk.

*"Lyrics,"* hissed Resus. "No one can remember the *lyrics!*"

"I can," said Tee quietly.

"You can what?"

"I can remember the lyrics to 'Zombie Feasting Time.'"

"Even though you only heard it once, back in Scream Street?" asked Cleo.

Tee nodded. "I'm pretty sure I've got it all."

"OK," said Resus disbelievingly. "Let's try again."

This time when the musicians started playing, everyone was amazed to hear Tee's powerful voice ringing out:

*If I rip the heart right from your chest,*
*They'll take me away; cardiac arrest. . . ."*

Green smoke began to swirl around Jazpants and Twonk.

*"I'll let your blood flow like a river,*
*Mop it all up with your juicy liver."*

As Tee sang, the emerald mist rose higher and higher.

After a few more bars of music there was a flash, and the tennis racket and sticks fell to the ground. Jazpants and Twonk had gone.

"It worked!" shouted Luke, clapping Tee on the back.

"Where did you learn to sing like that?" asked Cleo.

Tee shrugged. "It suddenly came back to me that I liked music," he said. "Maybe music was one of the things I was into when I was alive?"

"Then why didn't you just disappear like the other two?"

"I don't know," admitted Tee. "Maybe it works on those already affected by the spell first?"

Resus remained unconvinced. "It all seems a bit convenient to me," he grumbled, grabbing a log from the woodpile and throwing it on the fire.

Cleo glared at him. "Resus, no!"

The vampire squared up to her. "I'm entitled to my opinion, Cleo."

"I didn't mean that," shouted the mummy, plunging her hand into the fire and snatching the log back out. "This isn't a piece of wood. It's a leg!"

Crimson dawn was breaking by the time Luke found the head. "It's definitely Porridge," he confirmed, gingerly picking up the zombie's skull by the hair. He jumped as the creature's eyes flickered open and gazed up at him.

"This is pretty cool of you, buddy," said Porridge. "I just haven't been feeling myself lately."

"Probably because you've been scattered all

over the Underlands," said Luke as he placed the head next to the rest of the collected body parts.

"OK, have we got everything now?" asked Resus, producing a needle and thread from his cloak. "Where do we start?"

"By paying attention in Dr. Skully's classes," groaned Cleo as she tried to fit the zombie's ribs into his spinal column. The bones fell to the ground with a clatter.

"Let's take it one step at a time," said Luke. "Tee, you stand there and act as a reference guide. Now, the head definitely goes on the shoulders . . ."

"Don't forget the neck," said Resus, handing over a cylinder of rotting flesh.

"Thanks!" Luke said with a gulp, gingerly taking it from him. He sat down on a blackened rock and slipped the neck over the top of the spine, placing the head on top of that and pushing the needle deep into the zombie's skin.

"Aaargh!" Porridge screamed in agony, causing Luke to topple backward off the rock. When he reappeared, Brain Drain's bass player was giggling.

"Sorry, dude," Porridge said, grinning. "Couldn't resist!"

# Chapter Nine
# The Fairy

**Luke's stomach churned** as he stitched the zombie back together. Every time he slid the needle into the scab-covered skin, rivers of pus oozed from the holes.

Resus and Cleo followed the lines of Tee's body to set out the parts of Porridge on the ground like a jigsaw puzzle. They handed each bone, organ, or flap of flesh to Luke as required.

Eventually the job was finished and Porridge stood before them, whole once more. "Well," he said, smiling, "how do I look?"

"There's something not quite right," said Resus thoughtfully. "Don't go to pieces, but you seem all out of proportion."

"You've mixed his arms and legs up," groaned Cleo.

"*I've* mixed them up?" said Luke. "*You* were the one telling me which order to sew things in!"

Porridge gazed down at his new body. His arms were stitched to the bottom of his torso, with his feet attached to his wrists. The zombie's long legs hung down from his shoulders, fingers where his toes should be.

"We'll have to take them off and redo them," Resus said with a sigh.

"No!" protested Porridge. "I like it this way."

"But you look like an orangutan," said Luke. "Your knuckles are scraping along the ground!"

"Yes," the zombie said with a smile. "But imagine how cool I'll look with my bass guitar strapped so low around my neck! I thank you for your assistance."

"Now we just have to get you back to Scream Street," said Resus.

"We'll need something to stand in as a bass guitar," said Luke. "But what?"

Cleo unwound a length of bandage from her leg. "If you stand on one end of this and hold it taut, that might sound like a bass."

Porridge shook his head. "I'm afraid that won't work," he said. "I always play an electric bass guitar. What you're suggesting would be more like an upright double bass."

"Suit yourself, then," shrugged Cleo, beginning to wrap the bandage back around her leg.

Porridge smiled. "With a few small alterations, however . . ."

"I feel utterly stupid," said Cleo, grimacing.

Resus bit his lip and tried hard not to laugh. "You look great, though—doesn't she, Luke?"

Luke turned away to hide his smile. "Don't involve me in this," he said. Cleo was hanging sideways around Porridge's neck by a length of bandage, another strip strung from her shoulder to her foot. She was a living bass guitar.

"It'll only be for a few minutes," said Tee

88

kindly, "and you'll be helping
a lot."

"Stay rigid, now," said
Resus, with a grin. Cleo
glared at him.

"OK," said
Porridge, flexing
his fingers. "I'm
ready."

Tee closed his eyes
and began to sing.
*"If I rip the heart right from
your chest . . ."*

Porridge plucked at his
makeshift bass in time to the
song. Within seconds, the
green gas swirled up around his
feet. Cleo crashed to the ground as the zombie
vanished into the mist.

"Well," said the mummy. "Isn't someone
going to help me up?"

Resus, Luke, and Tee were in fits of giggles.

"It's not funny!" yelled Cleo.

"I know," Luke said, wheezing and clutching
his sides.

"Then there's no need to grin quite so widely, OK?"

"Oh, yes, there is!" screamed a voice. With a bloodcurdling yell, a large woman in an off-white leotard and tutu launched herself from the branches of the tree above and tackled Luke to the ground. Fumbling at a tool belt stitched into the waistband of her tutu, the woman grabbed a hammer and swung it toward his mouth.

"Oh, no," shouted Resus. "It's the Tooth Fairy!"

Luke turned his face to one side just in time as the hammer plunged into the black sand beside his head. The fairy tried to pull it out again, but the hammer was buried too deep. She snatched up a wrench from her tool belt instead and grinned.

"Smile for the last time, pretty boy," she screeched. "Those pearly whites *will* be mine!"

Before she could go for Luke again, Resus threw himself at the fairy, knocking her aside. Tee stamped on her wrist, forcing her to release the wrench. Cleo tossed it out of reach.

"You fools," squealed the fairy. "This is my only chance to escape!"

Luke scrambled away across the sand. "How? By caving my face in?"

"They said that I was neglecting my duties," ranted the Tooth Fairy. "That some little brats had woken up with their teeth still under their pillows instead of money. But I'll show them. I'll show them all!" Snatching a rock from the ground, she hurled it at Luke, catching him on the shoulder.

"You're insane!" he roared.

The Tooth Fairy nodded, her belly wobbling with the sudden movement. "That's what they said when I asked for a second chance. They sent me here—they said they'd find a replacement. But I'll be back! All I need is some teeth . . ."

With this the fairy ran at Luke, throwing herself on top of him and pinning his arms to the ground. Eyes flashing crazily, she raised her head and brought it down hard against Luke's mouth, splitting his lip.

Resus and Tee pulled the crazed woman off their friend. "Stop this," pleaded Cleo. "You can't just take teeth: they have to fall out first!"

"Dental matters might just be the least of our worries," warned Resus.

Luke clutched at his face as the pain from his lip rocketed through his skull. He felt his eyeballs swell, a yellow film coating them as the full force of his transformation hit him. His face stretched out to form a snout, and long, sharp teeth burst from his gums. Soon he was entirely covered in thick brown fur.

The werewolf stood and howled at the blood-red sky.

"Why's he so big?" said Cleo. "I don't remember him being so big before!"

"It must be the effect of the Underlands," guessed Resus. "It's made him into a monster." He flashed a glance at the Tooth Fairy and saw the fanatical smile vanish from her face. "He'll tear her apart!"

"So?" replied Cleo. "She attacked him first. Why should we help her?"

"*She's* clearly mad," said Resus, pointing to the fairy. "Luke isn't!"

"I don't know," said Cleo. "He looks pretty mad to me!"

Resus stepped in front of the werewolf. "Luke," he said. "I know you're in there, and I want you to listen to me. Leave the fairy alone."

The werewolf roared with rage and lashed out, knocking Resus to the ground with a powerful paw. The creature leaped around to where the Tooth Fairy cowered and lunged toward her stomach, jaws open wide.

Tearing away the tool belt, the wolf hurled it aside and growled down at the sobbing fairy, saliva dripping onto her leotard from his tongue. "I'm s—sorry," she stammered. "I just needed some teeth."

Tee ran at Luke, grabbing the werewolf around the waist and dragging it away from the terrified woman. "Get rid of her!" he shouted to

Resus and Cleo, fighting to keep his hold on the beast.

Resus scrambled to his feet, and pulling his false fangs out of his mouth, he thrust them into the Tooth Fairy's trembling hand. "Take these," he said. "Just get as far away from here as you can!"

"Resus, you can't," shouted Cleo.

"I can," replied Resus. "I'm not a real vampire — I don't need them." He swung back to face the fairy, glaring fiercely. "Go!"

Nodding, the fairy struggled to her feet, then flapped her wings and soared into the air, not looking back once as she disappeared over the treetops.

"OK, now there's just the rabid, snarling wolf to deal with," said Resus.

The werewolf hooked its claws around Tee's shoulders and flipped him over. With a flash of glistening teeth, it bit deep into the zombie's arm.

"Tee!" The wolf spun around to face Cleo, advancing slowly. "Luke, it's us," she said, tears running down her cheeks. "Your friends!"

"He can't hear us; he's in too deep," said

Resus, taking Cleo's hand. "There's nothing we can do."

"But it can't end like this," cried the mummy. "Not now, not here!"

The wolf took another step toward them and then its eyes widened as a *clang* blotted out the sound of its deep-throated growl. As Luke collapsed to the ground, unconscious, Resus and Cleo saw Vein standing behind him, the fairy's metal wrench clutched in his hands.

"It's not ending here at all," drawled the singer.

# Chapter Ten
# The Return

**When Luke woke up** he found himself tied to a tree stump. He struggled to free himself but the bandages were too tight.

"How are you feeling?" asked Resus, coming over.

"Human again," said Luke. "Can you untie me?"

"Leave him where he is!" Vein appeared behind the vampire. "If you let him go, he could rip out our throats."

Luke stared up at the singer. "What are you doing here?" he asked. "And what are you talking about?"

"You bit Tee," said Cleo.

Luke paled. "Is he all right?"

"I'm fine," said Tee, stepping into view. His arm was in a sling made from another of Cleo's bandages.

"I don't understand," said Luke, bewildered. "I've never attacked my friends before."

"It's the Underlands," said Resus. "This place affects you."

"Don't tell me," groaned Luke. "Negative energy, right?" Resus nodded.

"Which is exactly why we can't let him go," insisted Vein.

Resus shook his head. "I trust him."

"Fine, have it your way," snapped the singer, snatching up the metal wrench.

Resus quickly untied Luke's bonds. "Talk to

him," he hissed. "He's been like this for hours! It's driving me nuts."

Luke calmly approached the zombie. "It's OK," he said, holding out his hands to show he meant no harm. "It only happens when I get angry, and that's over now."

"Why did you follow us here?" asked Vein. "To this place?"

"I need the relic you left behind as a founding father of Scream Street."

"You need my tongue?" asked Vein.

"Yes," said Luke. "I have to take my parents. . . . Wait a minute. The relic is your *tongue*? The actual tongue you've got in your mouth at this moment?"

Vein nodded.

Luke took a deep breath. "I need it to open a doorway back to my world."

"Well, you can't have it," snarled Vein. "I'm the lead singer in the world's greatest zombie rock band. Giving you my tongue would end my career."

"But . . . you offered it as a relic to help those who follow," said Luke. "Changing your mind now would just be selfish!"

"I'm not the one being selfish here," said Vein. "Before I joined Brain Drain, I was a nobody with nothing to look forward to in death. I will not go back to that!"

Luke blinked back tears of frustration as the zombie turned and stalked away.

Cleo put an arm around him. "You OK?"

"It's over," declared Luke.

"You don't know that," said Resus. "Maybe you only need the relics from the founding fathers who are prepared to give them to you."

Luke pulled *Skipstone's Tales of Scream Street* from his pocket and looked expectantly at the silver cover. "I'm afraid not," said Skipstone. "All six relics are required to access the power of the founding fathers."

"Could *you* talk to Vein?" Cleo asked the author.

Skipstone shook his head. "The fathers must give their gifts freely, or not at all. There is nothing I can do."

Luke sighed, tucking the book away again. "Let's just go home," he said.

"Er, I've been meaning to talk to you about that," said Resus.

Cleo stared at the vampire. "Tell me you're not about to say that we came here without a plan to get home."

"I didn't expect us to get this far," said Resus defensively. "We found that Hex Hatch by accident, and then everything happened so quickly . . ."

"What about the Hex Hatch?" asked Luke. "Could we use it to get back?"

"Possibly," said Resus. "But I've no idea how we'd find it among the clouds, or how we could get up there even if we did."

"So, basically, we're stuck here," said Cleo.

"Well, I do have one idea . . ."

"Hello, Underlands!" called Vein, using a stick as a makeshift microphone.

"This will never work," muttered Cleo as she plucked at the length of bandage stretched between her hips and wrist.

"It might," said Resus, tapping on the pans in front of him with a dead twig. "The spell shouldn't be able to tell that we're not the real band!"

"What do you think happens," asked Luke,

tennis racket clutched in his hands, "when the green smoke appears?"

"Hopefully we're about to find out," said Resus as Vein finished his intro. Tee stood beside the older zombie, ready to sing along into the jar of glowworms.

"This is our latest song," announced Vein. "It's called 'Zombie Feasting T—'" He stopped. "Something's not right," he said.

"What?" asked Resus. "These pretend instruments worked for the other band members."

"It's not the instruments," said Vein. "You just don't *look* like musicians!" Tucking the stick into his pocket, Vein grabbed one of the tattoos stitched onto his arm and tore it off. Carrying the flap of flesh over to Cleo, he slapped it against her shoulder, where a mixture of mucus and pus held it in place.

"If we do get home," Cleo said through gritted teeth, "you'll be joining the undead, Resus Negative!"

Vein stared thoughtfully at Tee. "Your eyes are too bright," he said. "I have mine injected with black ink every couple of weeks."

"It's OK," called Resus as the shy young zombie flushed a paler shade of green. "I've got some sunglasses here!" He tossed the shades to Tee.

Vein looked at his new band. "Now we're ready," he said. "Except . . ."

Luke sighed. "Except what?"

"We haven't got an audience! We need to build up the right atmosphere."

Resus gazed around the vast empty plain. "It's been a while since this place had *any* atmosphere."

It took almost an hour for Luke, Resus, and Cleo to locate the Tooth Fairy and ask for her help—and another one to persuade her that the werewolf really had gone. "It's OK," Luke told her. "I know it wasn't personal."

Flying off, the fairy soon returned with the unicorn, two gargoyles, and a dozen or so monkeylike creatures with green spiked hair.

"There," said Resus. "How's that?"

Vein grinned as the band took up their positions once again. "We're back, Underlands," he shouted into his stick. "This is 'Zombie Feasting Time'!"

Resus battered away at his pots and pans. Luke

strummed the tennis racket, and Cleo plucked at her bandage.

*"If I rip the heart right from your chest,*
*They'll take me away; cardiac arrest. . . ."* sang Vein as Tee joined in with the harmonies.

Luke winced. The sound they were making was terrible! Even the green-haired monkeys were running away in terror. Surely no one could be tricked into thinking that they were a real—

A dense green gas began to bubble up around his feet. Luke looked from pretend musician to pretend musician and saw that they, too, were gradually being enveloped in the smoke.

"It's working!" he shouted. There was a flash of green light, then Luke found himself flying through a swirling emerald tunnel. Someone whooped with joy and Luke turned to see Resus beside him, his cape flapping out from his shoulders.

Then Cleo appeared. "I'll get you for this, Resus!" she screamed.

Finally Vein and Tee arrived, laughing helplessly. "This is just like the first time," called the singer. "Get ready for a bumpy landing."

Another burst of green light filled the air, and Luke landed with a thud on the stage in Central Square of Scream Street. Jazpants stood beside him and appeared to be in the middle of a guitar solo. Incredibly, it seemed that although they had spent the night in the Underlands, only a few minutes had passed in Scream Street.

Resus arrived next and found himself sitting at the drum kit beside Twonk. "Now, *that's* funny!" the drummer said, his face beaming, as the vampire joined in with his own sticks.

Porridge seemed to be having a great time, his stumpy new legs planted firmly on the stage and his bass guitar slung low below his waist. Then there was a crack of green lightning and Cleo landed squarely on the zombie's shoulders.

"Welcome back, little lady." Porridge smiled as Cleo screamed in surprise.

A final flash of light burst into view at the front of the stage. As it cleared, Vein and Tee could be seen standing together, singing the song into real microphones.

*"I'll let your blood flow like a river,*
*Mop it all up with your juicy liver!"*

The zombies in the audience roared with delight as their hero reappeared.

*"Chewing on you, you're tasting good,*
*Gnawing your bones and tasting blood.*
*I chews you—it's zombie feasting time!"*

Luke grinned at Cleo and Resus. Maybe the fact that Vein didn't want to hand over his tongue wasn't so bad after all. Moments like this made life in Scream Street enjoyable—perhaps he could even convince his mom and dad to get to know their neighbors. Maybe then they'd—

Luke's thoughts were suddenly interrupted by a commotion behind him.

"Stop this right now!" Sir Otto, purple with fury, charged onto the stage. One by one the musicians stopped playing, until silence filled the square.

"What are you all doing here?" roared the landlord. "I banished you to the Underlands!"

# Chapter Eleven
# The Relic

**"Dude!" called a voice** from the front of the crowd. Doug flipped open the top of his head to scratch his brain. *"You* sent them there?"

"It's true," said Vein, pointing to Sir Otto. "This man sent us to the worst place you could ever imagine."

At this, the zombies around Doug lunged forward with a screech and grabbed Sir Otto's ankles. The landlord fell with a crash as the creatures dragged him off the stage and into the crowd. Within seconds they were all over him.

Luke raced to the front of the stage and snatched the microphone from Vein's hands. "Stop!" he commanded.

The zombies paused and turned to face the stage. Luke swallowed hard and spoke nervously into the microphone. "Sir Otto Sneer is a bad man," he said. "He does bad things to a lot of people—but that doesn't mean you should hurt him for it."

Doug pushed his way back to the front of the crowd. "The little dude's right!" he said.

"What's happened to the spirit of Deadstock?" The zombies looked quizzically at one another for a second, then, with a mass roar, they pushed Doug to one side and continued their attack on the unfortunate landlord.

"So much for the diplomatic approach," said Resus, reaching inside his cloak. "Time for something a little more persuasive!" With that, he pulled out a squirming cloth sack and ripped away the cord from around its neck. Dozens of angry pixies flew out of the bag and shot into the crowd, biting and scratching everything in sight.

The zombies at the front howled in pain. Dropping Sir Otto, they began to retreat across the square.

Staggering and lurching back up the side

streets and into the yards nearby, the zombies dived into the tunnels that had brought them to Scream Street in the first place. The pixies gave chase, darting from monster to monster, snapping their razor-sharp teeth.

"You brought those things back from the Underlands?" demanded Cleo, joining Resus and Luke at the front of the stage.

"I figured they might come in handy."

The trio leaped down from the stage and fought their way through the retreating crowd to Sir Otto. The landlord lay curled up in a ball on the ground, sobbing like a baby.

"Let's get you out of here," said Luke, grabbing one of Sir Otto's wrists as Resus pulled the other.

Cleo lifted up the flap of cloth that hung across the front of the stage so the boys could drag Sir Otto away from the stampede. Turning, she found herself faced with the gray, one-eyed zombie once again. "What now?" she said.

The creature gave a gentle moan and handed Cleo a single dead flower. Then, sighing heavily, he turned and limped slowly away toward his tunnel.

"You know," said Cleo as she joined Luke, Resus, and a trembling Sir Otto beneath the stage, "I've really changed my opinion of zombies!"

"And I've changed my opinion of were-wolves," said a voice. Luke spun around to find Vein crawling under the stage toward them.

"I was worried about what giving you my relic would do to me," admitted the zombie. "What I didn't consider is what you would do for others."

"What do you mean?" asked Luke.

Vein gestured toward Sir Otto. "You saved this man, even though he tried to take everything from you! That's the bravest thing I've ever seen; it made me realize that I need to be brave too."

Opening his mouth, Vein grabbed hold of his tongue and pulled. With a sickening squelch, the muscle tore away. *"Ih i or ooh,"* he mumbled, handing over the quivering chunk of flesh.

"But—the band!" said Luke. "Your career . . ."

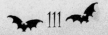

"Vein is going to be the band's manager from now on," said Tee, appearing beside them. "They've got a new singer."

"You?" exclaimed Cleo, throwing her arms around her new friend. "But what happened to finding out who you really are?"

"I know who I am now," Tee said with a smile. "I'm a zombie."

"If this gets any mushier, I think I might throw up." Resus grinned, pretending to be sick.

"Sneer's gone!" exclaimed Luke, interrupting him.

Sir Otto was nowhere to be seen. Resus lifted the cloth in time to see the landlord scurrying away toward the gates of Sneer Hall. "I guess he just about gets away with it—this time."

"I suppose so," agreed Luke.

"Er, not quite," admitted Cleo. "While you were busy taking pixies from the Underlands, I was leaving something behind . . ."

"What?" Luke asked cautiously. There was a flash of green light and a heavy thud shook the stage above them.

"I wrote down the lyrics to 'Zombie Feasting Time,'" said the mummy with a grin. "The Tooth

112

Fairy must have found them somehow and joined in with the song."

"Whoa, mama!" bellowed the Tooth Fairy, leaping to the ground and chasing after Sir Otto. "Let me get a look at those pearly whites!"

"You gave the Tooth Fairy her freedom?" asked Resus.

Cleo nodded. "In return for these," she said, opening her hand.

"My fangs!" exclaimed Resus, snatching them up from her hands.

"Well," said Cleo, "what's a vampire without them?"

"Still no sign of the pixies," said Luke as he unfastened a section of the stage and handed it to Porridge.

"I think they must have followed the zombies into the tunnels," said Resus. "With any luck, they'll fly into a Hex Hatch and wind up back in the Underlands."

"I hope it's not the same one we'll be using to get this stuff to our next gig," said Jazpants, loading another piece of the stage onto the tour bus.

"Where's your next concert?" asked Cleo.

"Norway," replied the zombie. "We've got a huge following among the trolls."

"They're funny!" said Twonk, lumbering over with a pile of drum cases. "I bet they'll love our new lead simper, too."

"Lead *singer*!" shouted everyone together.

"Oh, yeah!"

"Speaking of which," added Porridge, "where is the little guy?"

"Here," said Tee, emerging from the doors of Everwell's Emporium. "Vein's been helping me find a new look," he added shyly. The young zombie twirled around to show off his new leather jacket, ripped jeans, and scarlet bandanna.

"You're the best-dressed zombie I've ever seen," Luke said with a grin.

"These are yours," said Tee, handing the sunglasses back to Resus.

The vampire shook his head. "You keep them," he said, smiling. "Unless you want to end up a slave to injections like old inky-eyes over there!"

Vein smiled languidly and made a rude gesture with his hand. Cleo giggled. "I guess he doesn't need a tongue to say what he thinks!"

"OK, guys," shouted Porridge as he finished loading the last item onto the tour bus. "Everyone on board. We've got trolls waiting!"

"Give me a minute," said Tee as the rest of the band climbed onto the bus. Vein nodded and waved his good-byes as he clambered aboard.

"I want you to have this," said Tee, handing Cleo a parcel.

"What is it?" asked the mummy.

Tee smiled. "Something to remember me by."

Cleo blinked back tears. Resus put his arm around her as Tee stepped up onto the bus and the doors closed. Revving up the engine, Vein drove the bus across Scream Street's Central Square. As the vehicle hit the invisible Hex Hatch, it disappeared.

Cleo tore open the parcel to discover Tee's original mud-stained jacket. The embroidered *T* now had another letter beside it: *C*.

"I don't think you'll have any problem remembering him," said Resus, hugging the sobbing mummy. "Hey," he added as Cleo's tears splashed onto his cape. "You're showering me!"

"Showering!" Luke's face paled, and he ran across the square in the direction of his house.

"Where's he going in such a hurry?" Cleo said, sniffling.

Resus grinned. "His mom and dad are still locked in the bathroom!"

**Tommy Donbavand** was born and raised in Liverpool, England, and has held a variety of jobs, including clown, actor, theater producer, children's entertainer, drama teacher, storyteller, and writer. His nonfiction books for children and their parents, *Boredom Busters* and *Quick Fixes for Bored Kids,* have helped him to become a regular guest on radio stations around the U.K. He also writes for a number of magazines, including *Creative Steps* and Scholastic's *Junior Education Plus*.

Tommy sees the Scream Street series as what might have resulted had Stephen King been a writer for *Scooby Doo*. "Writing the Scream Street books is fangtastic fun," he says. "I just have to be careful not to scare myself too much!" Tommy lives in England with his family and sees sleep as a waste of good writing time.

You can find out more about Tommy and his books at his website: www.tommydonbavand.com.